Divorced Together

For the Sake of the Children

Written and Illustrated by

Kristi Schwartz

Ferne Press

Divorced Together for the Sake of the Children
Copyright © 2010 by Kristi Schwartz
Illustrated by Kristi Schwartz
Printed in Canada

Summary: Colin and Allie realize that their parents' divorce doesn't change their lives in a bad way.

Library of Congress Cataloging-in-Publication Data
    Schwartz, Kristi
    Divorced Together for the Sake of the Children / Kristi Schwartz – First Edition
    ISBN-13: 978-1-933916-47-7
    1. Co-parenting after divorce. 2. Divorce. 3. Juvenile Fiction. 4. Elementary school fiction.
    I. Schwartz, Kristi II. Divorced Together for the Sake of the Children
    Library of Congress Control Number: 2009934623

FERNE PRESS

Ferne Press is an imprint of Nelson Publishing & Marketing
366 Welch Road, Northville, MI 48167
www.nelsonpublishingandmarketing.com
(248) 735-0418

This book is dedicated to the two little ones that are my positive ray of sunshine through any difficult experience: Colin and Allie. Thank you for always being my inspiration. You both bring out the best in me, and I am a better person today for having you in my life.

This book would not be possible without all of the love and support of my close family and friends. I want to thank Amy and Mom for believing in my dreams as much as I do. For giving me the environment to create in, I want to thank my husband, Keith. Julie, Kerri, and Katrina were always there to listen to my ideas and encourage me. Marian and Kris have given me this opportunity, and the insight to make my dream come true.

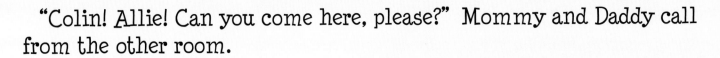

"Colin! Allie! Can you come here, please?" Mommy and Daddy call from the other room.

"Colin, they look serious," Allie says.
"Mommy and Daddy love you both so much, and you will always be first in our lives. But we now are going to live in separate homes." Mommy says.
"Are you getting a divorce?" Colin asks.
Mommy and Daddy say, "Yes."

Daddy explains, "Sometimes it's hard for mommies and daddies to live in the same house, and it's better if they live in separate homes. But we will both be available for you, no matter what."

Mommy wraps her arms around both of them and swipes each forehead with a kiss.

"Remember the beautiful flowers that we have at the side of our house? The ones with the purple blossoms and the gorgeous fragrance?"

"At one time, these flowers were all at Grandma and Grandpa's house."

"They're my favorite!" Allie exclaims.

"Grandpa gave me some of the plants. With my love and care, they grow bigger and bigger each year, and the blossoms are more plentiful and gorgeous."

"Sometimes, the same is true with families, and they just need to be rearranged in order to grow and flourish. The nice thing about families is that their love grows bigger and more beautiful each day. This is a good way to describe divorce." Mommy leads them outside to see the flowers.

"See?" Mommy asks. "These flowers are more beautiful than last year at this time."

"They are taller than Daddy now," Colin notices.

"You're right. Close your eyes and take a deep breath. Do you smell the wonderful fragrance, even though you don't see the flowers? Even if you can't see me, I am always here for you, no matter what," Mommy explains.

"Hey, would you like to go see your second home?" Daddy asks.

"I think that you two need some bright, fragrant flowers for your home with Daddy. Do you want to take some of Grandpa's flowers with you?" Mommy asks.

Colin and Allie yell, "Yes!"

"Whenever you see Grandpa's flowers, they will remind you about our family, our love, our homes...no matter where Mommy or Daddy are."

Daddy adds, "We are always going to be together for you both—our family is one huge flower garden. Our plants are simply in different places."

Colin and Allie wake up at their new house with Daddy. They trudge out to the breakfast table.

"I miss Mommy singing the 'Wake Up' song, Colin," Allie says.

"Me too, Allie."

The door bursts open and Daddy charges in, singing,
"Good morning to Colin, good morning to you!
Good morning to Allie, good morning to you!"
"Mommy must have taught him the song," guesses Colin.
Daddy replies, "Why yes, she did."

Mommy takes Colin and Allie
to the park. "The climber is not
fun," Colin sighs.

Mommy asks, "You don't want
to go on the swings?"

"But...who will push me?"
asks Colin.

With a quirky smile, Mommy
looks at Colin.

"Who do you think?"

They run to the swings, where Mommy pushes them higher than ever.

"Daddy must have taught her how to push us high on the swings," guesses Allie. Mommy replies, "Why yes, he did."

At Colin's swim meet, Daddy drops him off at the boys' locker room and finds a seat in the bleachers with Allie.

Mommy and Daddy used to come to the swim meet together. Today, Daddy takes Colin and Allie to the meet alone.

Colin curls his toes around the front of the starting block, waiting for the announcer to start the race.

"On your mark, get set, GO!" the announcer chants.

"Go Colin!" yells Daddy.

"You can do it, Mr. Colin!" screams Mommy.

After Colin crosses the finish line, he rips off his goggles to see Allie sandwiched between Mommy and Daddy in the bleachers. Mommy came to watch him swim, too.

"That's even better than winning!" whispers Colin to himself.

It's dance recital time, and Mommy packs up to go to the auditorium.

Daddy and Mommy always used to go to the recital together. Today, Mommy takes Allie and Colin to the recital alone.

Backstage, Mommy puts makeup on Allie for the performance. She snaps pictures of the dancing beauty from every angle.

"Okay, Bumblebees, it's time to line up," the assistant calls.

When Allie gets in line, she feels the famous "Daddy Backwards Hug."

"Daddy!" Allie screams.

When she turns around, he has a bouquet of the special purple flowers with him. "You came to my recital!"

"Well, don't bees like flowers? I have to watch my little bumblebee buzz," he teases.

Fall is in the air, and October is finally here. It's birthday time.
"Will Daddy still come over for our birthdays?" Colin asks Allie, while
they clean their rooms for the party.

Allie sighs, "I hope so. Our family is always together for our birthdays."

Colin
♡ Grandma
Grandpa

"Happy Birthday, Colin and Allie!" shouts Daddy, along with the grandmas and grandpas, and the aunts and uncles.

"Look, Colin! Both grandmas and grandpas are here!" Allie exclaims.

"Yeah! Like always!" Colin replies.

"What did you wish for? Wait! Don't tell me...it won't come true." whispers Colin.

"It already did, Colin.
It already did!"

Epilogue

Divorce can be a devastating dilemma that affects many families. Often in a divorce situation, people may feel that many decisions are out of their control. It's up to each person in a divorce to control their emotions. If children are involved, each adult needs to set their own emotions aside and make decisions that are in the best interest of the children.

Putting all differences aside provides a positive environment for any home. Divorce homes are not "broken" homes, unless that is the path chosen. A divorce does not break a home—the lack of a solid foundation does.

This book is meant to show that not all divorce situations are negative. There can be positive aspects in a divorce. Practicing kindness toward each other, while relating to the children, builds a positive foundation for this significant change in the children's lives. The needs of the children must be the main priority. Kindness breeds kindness, in any situation.

About the Author

Kristi Schwartz resides in Canton, Michigan with her two children, Colin and Allie, her new husband, Keith, and their newborn, Drew. Currently an elementary teacher, Kristi has been teaching for ten years. Growing up, she was one of six children and she currently has seventeen nieces and nephews. Consequently, she experiences many dynamics of a family. In her free time, Kristi enjoys volunteering at the Farmington Players, a local community theater.